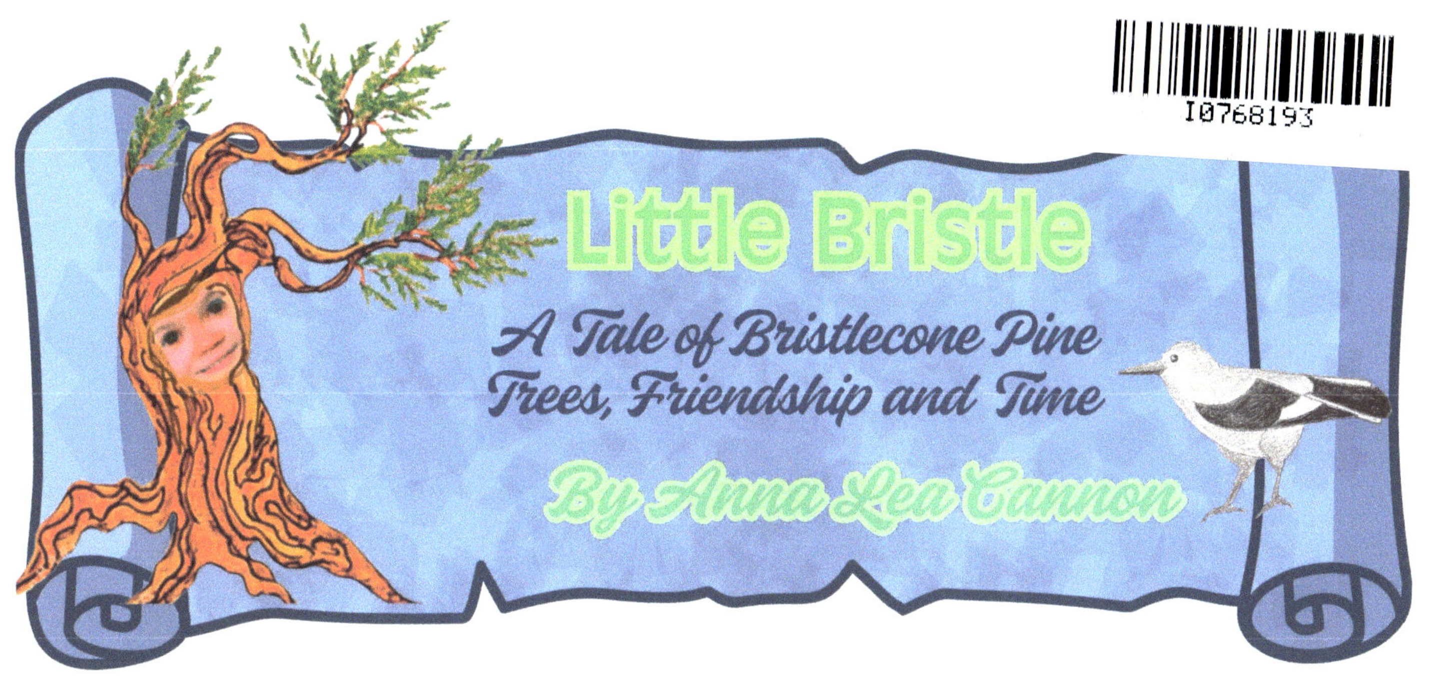

Copyright © 2025 by Annalea Cannon

ISBN: 978-1-968970-84-0 (sc)
ISBN: 978-1-968970-85-7 (e)

Inquiries and Book Orders should be addressed to:

Leavitt Peak Press
17901 Pioneer Blvd Ste L #298, Artesia, California 90701
Phone #: 2092191548

Little Bristle & Clarky:
A Tale of Friendship
and Time
1

Little Bristle slowly stretched and glanced around her rocky surroundings. Bristle had slept through the long winter but now spring had sprung. That meant Bristle's friend Clarky would return. After forty years of being alone, Bristle finally had a friend!

Clarky had accidentally found Bristle when he'd flown under her rocky ledge alcove while looking for a safe place to stash his pine nuts.

Clarky loved his little old friend and thought it was so cute that she was fifty but still no taller than a tulip.

Bristle didn't know what a tulip was so Clarky showed her using pine nuts and cones to create a collage of the flower's shape.

Clarky was pushing her roots against some remaining ice when Clarky flew in. Bristle danced her needles in joy. Clarky was back!

Clarky was a Clark's Nutcracker jay who flew up to the
high elevations in the summer to harvest bristlecone pine
cones. He could hide 33,000 seeds all over the mountain and
not forget where they were. He was brilliant!

Bristle loved to watch as Clarky used his strong beak
to open the pine cones and get the nuts.
Clarky's favorite game was to see how
many seeds he could fit in his mouth at one time.
Last summer, Clarky made it to fifty seeds!
After playing the game, he stashed the seeds
in the back of Bristle's little alcove.

Clarky was also friends with three ancient, tall bristlecone pine trees that grew just above and behind Bristle's limestone alcove. These trees were more than old. They'd seen over 2,500 summers. Clarky promised that if Bristle grew just a few inches more she could look out of the alcove to see and talk to them. She could also see the beautiful mountain peaks in the day and millions of stars at night.

Clarky's "get bigger" pep talks included advice from the ancient trees.

Bristle should stretch her branches towards the reflected sunlight of the white limestone rocks outside the alcove and cling tightly to her double-layered pine needles that could keep gathering sunlight for thirty-five years.

Pushing her roots to the loose soil of nearby limestone cracks would also provide better moisture, warmth, and nutrients for growing.

Bristle worked hard at growing that summer, and succeeded! By her 42nd summer, Bristle welcomed Clarky by reaching out of the cave to catch him on her outer branches.

Bristle could finally
see the beauty of the
jagged mountain
peaks as Clarky
nestled into her pine
needles.

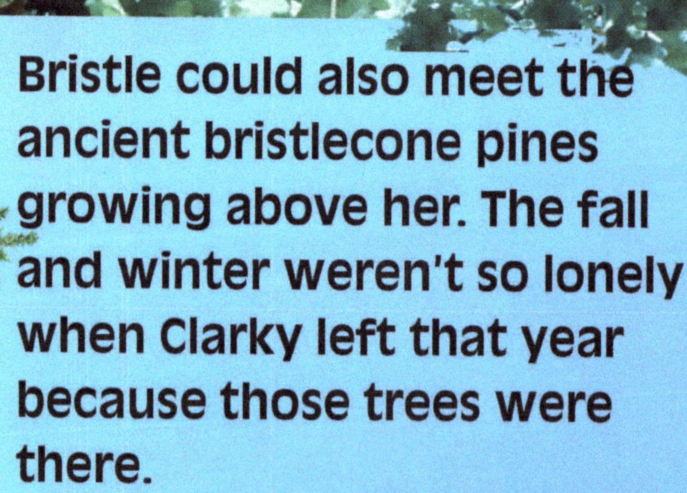

Bristle could also meet the
ancient bristlecone pines
growing above her. The fall
and winter weren't so lonely
when Clarky left that year
because those trees were
there.

11

They joked that 2,500 years was just middle-aged because several other trees on the mountain were over 5,000 years old. Word had it that they were older than the pyramids in Egypt -- Bristle didn't know what a pyramid in Egypt was but it was fun to think about.

Clarky surprised Bristle the following year by coming with his female mate and three chicks.

Bristle laughed as the chicks clumsily cracked open nuts from Clarky's stash on the little ledge. Bristle felt like a proud grandmother!

13

Year followed year, and Bristle's friend circle grew.

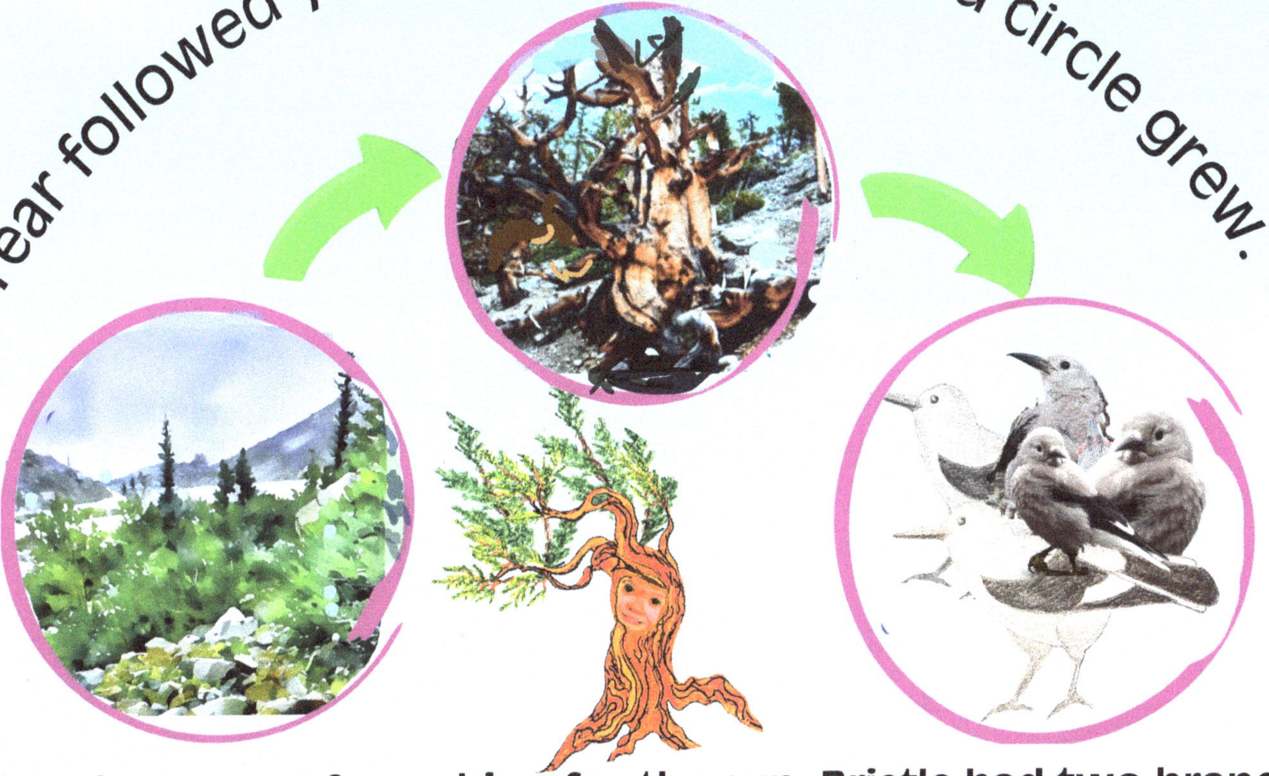

After five years of reaching for the sun, Bristle had two branches growing outside the alcove. She also grew purple pinecones that Clarky and his family moved here and there to make beautiful collages. The blue pine cones were inviting and warm like their friendship.

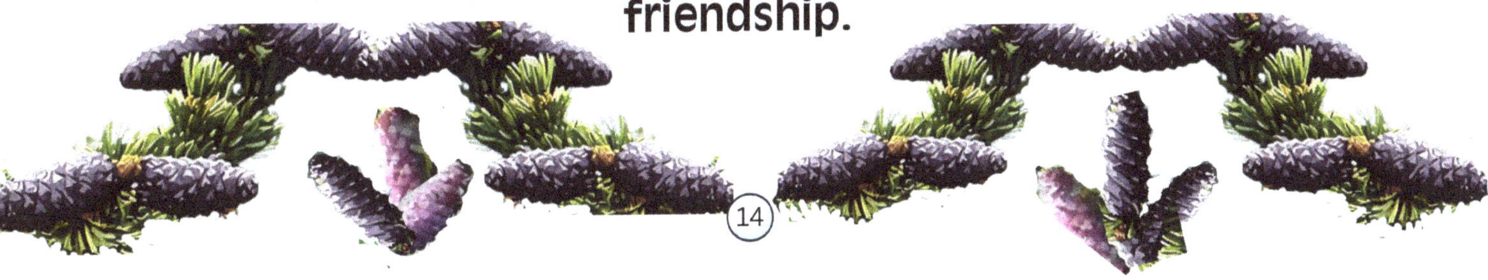

Clarky loved the quiet peace of the high elevation's vista in the summer, but even more he loved his good friend Bristle. He loved how the little tree had welcomed his family year after year.   He loved the way Bristle listened to his stories and kept his stash of pine nuts safe.

As for Bristle, it was amazing to have a friend like Clarky who came back summer after summer. They'd been friends now for 15 years. Bristle noticed that Clarky didn't flit from place to place as he had done before. He was content to stay still and talk. During one talk, Bristle was alarmed to learn that Clark's Nutcrackers only live 18 to 20 years. Bristle still had thousands of years to live, but Clarky was getting very old. What would Bristle do if he didn't come back?

Her worries increased when the winds blew so hard that they bent her branches, crashing them into the limestone rocks.

Snow and ice filled the cave wrapping her lower trunk and branches in a cold blanket even before she'd had a chance to fall asleep.

Months later, Bristle drowsily awakened to the sound of urgent pecking near her still snow-covered branches. Clarky was struggling to find the stash of pine nuts that was still packed with snow and ice. Spring had come early lower down the mountain but hadn't reached the high elevation yet. Clarky had been so anxious to see his friend that he had flown up the mountain much too early!

Suddenly, a giant gust of wind smashed the already weak bird toward the back of the alcove. There he lay completely still.

Now coming wide awake, Bristle tried frantically to pull her lower branches from the ice. Her branches didn't move. Next, she tried to wiggle free of a layer of snow that encased her upper branch. A sprinkling of snow fell on the dazed bird.

While this didn't help warm Clarky, it gave Bristle an idea. With great effort, Bristle shook snow off her branches and unclenched several of her best bunches of needles.

These needles were essential for Bristle's summer growth, but right then Bristle didn't care. She only wanted to save Clarky. Carefully, Bristle let her needles fall and blanket Clarky in their warmth.

After what seemed like hours,
Clarky finally moved!

Bristle could see pine nuts in the back of the cave that the ice had missed. She encouraged her friend to turn his head and eat the nuts, but Clarky couldn't move far. His wing was either frozen or broken.

Bristle dropped more of her double-thick pine needles atop Clarky, pushing aside any worries about how she would grow them back. Right now, Clarky needed warmth and healing!

Bristle distracted Clarky by asking about his adventures down the mountain. They joked about how Bristle was just a baby compared to the older trees. Their conversation and the warm pine needles helped Clarky stop shivering although his wing wasn't working. He hobbled closer to the stash of pine nuts pushing Bristle's warm needles with his mouth to make a cozy nest.

Night came and both friends slept. Bristle hoped her pine needles and the shelter of the alcove would warm her friend until they awakened in the morning, but . . .

...Bristle didn't wake up. Bristlecone pines remain dormant and sleep until the warmth and sunlight of summer comes

Clarky, on the other hand, awoke with pain but also gratitude. The pine needle nest was warming him and the pine nuts were giving him strength.

He counted many trees, birds, and other animals on the mountain as friends, but Bristle was a friend like no other. As he rested buried in Bristle's pine needles struggling for warmth, he thought of a way to say thank you to Bristle.

Nibbling on pine nuts for several days allowed him to think as more ice melted. Clarky couldn't fly with his broken wing but he could hop around.

He used some of the pine needles that had warmed him along with pine nuts to form the shape of a heart like a carving Clarky had seen on a tree lower down on the mountain.

While he worked Clarky also became determined to plant a bristlecone pine nearby to become Bristle's friend. Although his pain was rapidly worsening, he knew how to do it . . . He carefully filled his mouth with pine nuts,

and hobbled slowly to a wide crevice he knew had perfect conditions for growing a new bristlecone pine,

Moving aside the remaining snow, he dropped the pine nuts into the large crack. Then he laid down in the crack over the seeds to keep them warm and fell asleep. He never woke again.

Some weeks later, the spring sun warmed Bristle and sap started flowing back into her branches. She looked for Clarky. Instead, she found a beautiful collage in the alcove.

She recognized the pine needles she'd sacrificed for her friend and her . heart filled with love to see the intertwined stem of their friendship.

Their friendship had been short; yet, the memory and beauty of the friendship would be as endless as the life that still awaited her!

Bristle did lose a narrow strip of pine bark all the way up her trunk accompanied by a dead spot on the branch from which she had dropped needles to help Clarky.

In a few years a baby bristlecone pine sprouted out of a rock crevice in a perfect location not far from Bristle. It was now Bristle's turn to give growing advice and encouragement to her new friend.

Bristle wondered if it was possible that Clarky had planted the seed for this little tree. Even if he hadn't, Clarky had planted a seed of friendship that had multiplied into friendships with birds and trees throughout the forest.

What Does Old Mean for Bristlecone Pine Trees?

Bristlecone pine trees are the oldest trees in the world. One tree named Methuselah in Inyo National Forest in California is over 4,800 years old.

In 1964 a 5,000-year-old tree named Prometheus was cut down by scientists before they realized how old it was. As they cut away, they never dreamed they were chopping down a 5,000-year-old tree. This blunder made it so that the exact location of other ancient trees is kept secret.

Methusaleh is older than the Pyramid of Djoser in Egypt which was built in 2650 BCE, making it around 4,700 years old. The more famous pyramids of Giza in Egypt by Cairo were built 100 years later.

Older still is a plant clonal colony of quaking aspen in Fish Lake National Forest in Utah which is about 500 miles from Methusaleh.

This quaking aspen system called Pando looks like a forest but has connected roots that started growing over 14,000 years ago. Pando started with a single tree whose root system expanded and then shot up individual trees that now cover 106 acres.

Determining the Age of Pine Trees and Timeline

Dendrochronology is the study of counting tree rings to determine the exact age of trees. There are two basic ways to study the age of the tree. The first is to cut the tree down and count the rings. Doing this for Prometheus was disastrous.   The second way is to use an increment borer to gently drill to the center of the tree. After that a thin tube is placed in the middle of the borer and then pulled out again to see a tiny section of tree rings. This is generally safe for trees although bristlecone pine in National Forests are protected from even this safer method.

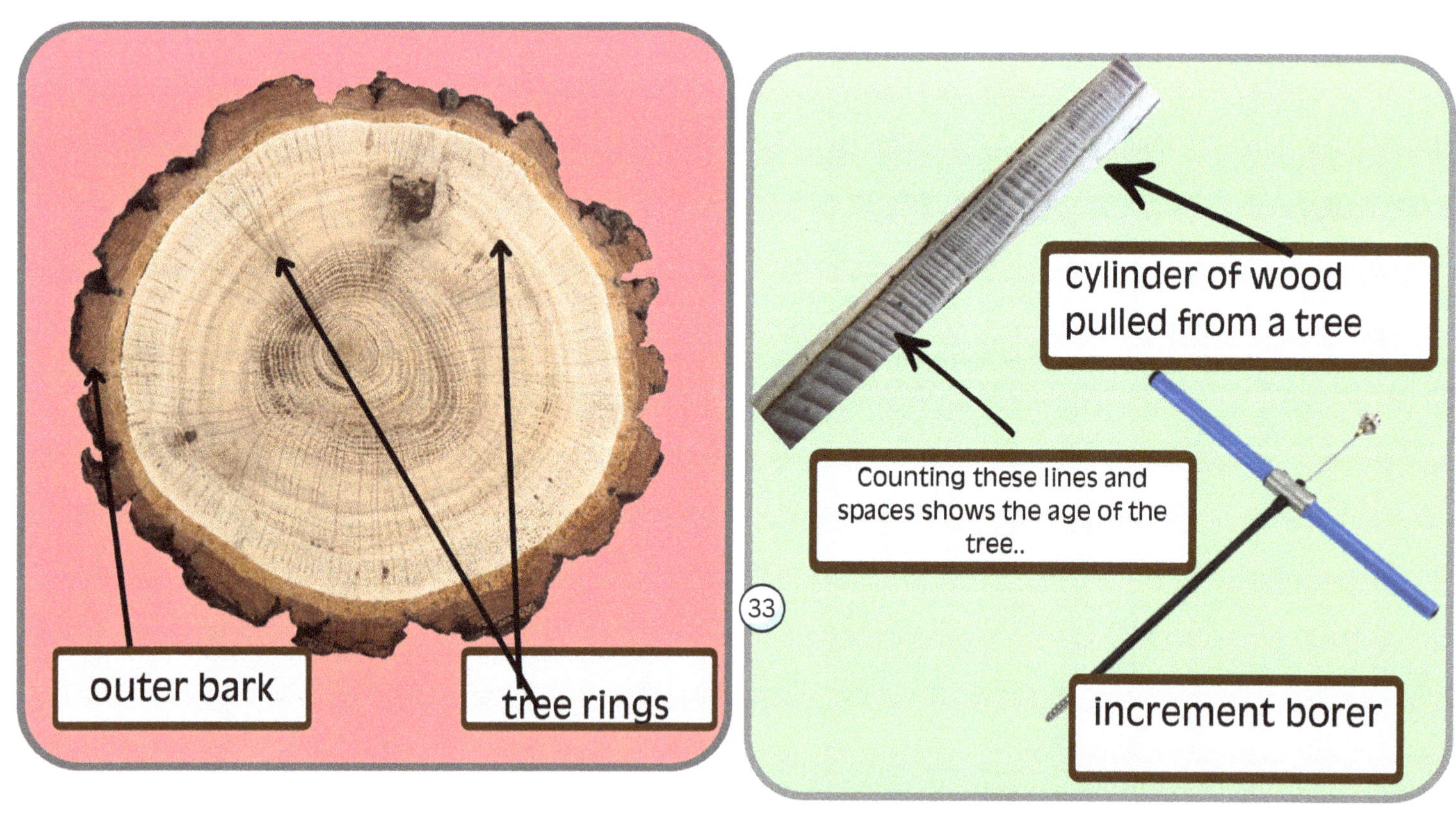

33

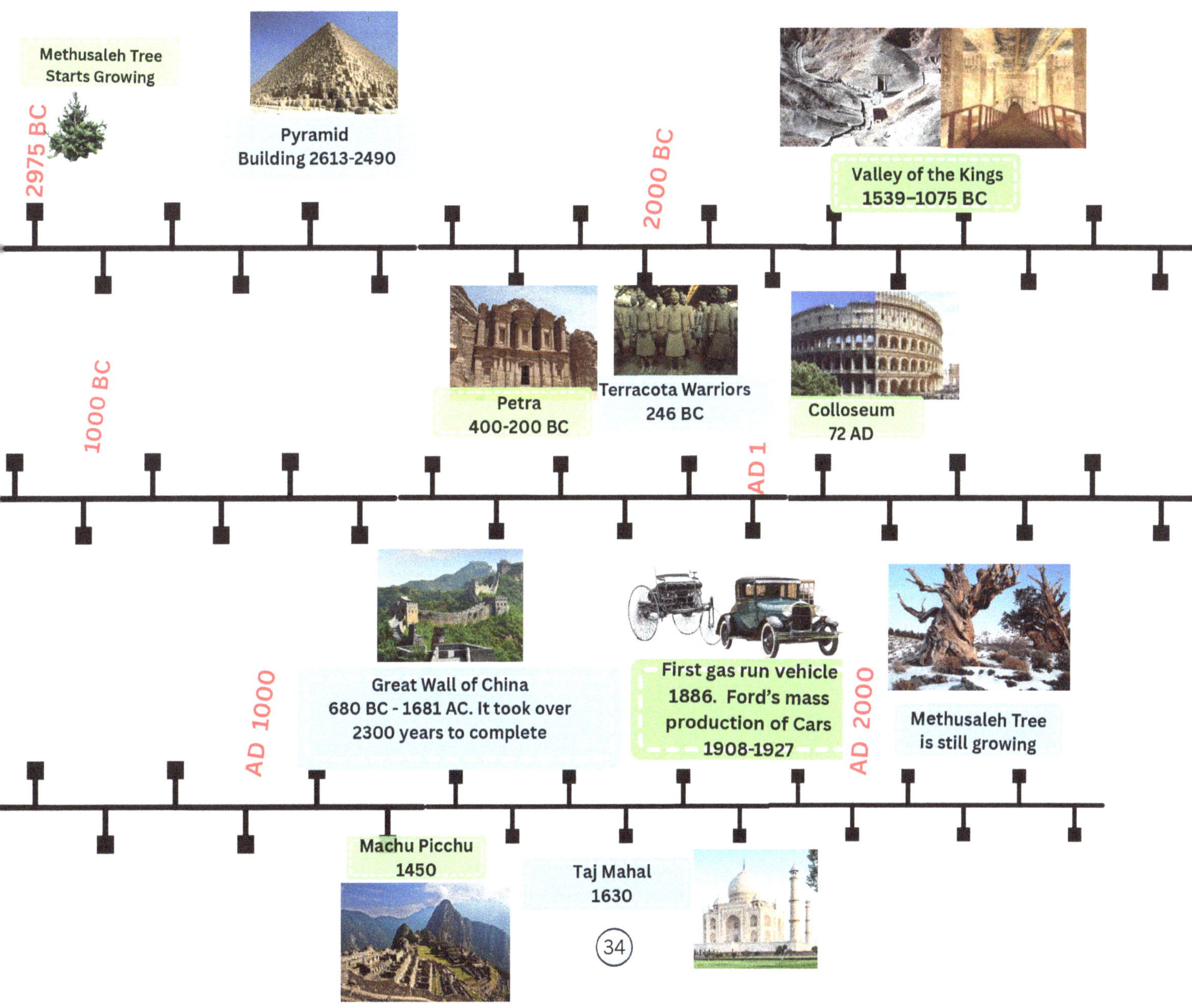

Methusaleh Tree
Starts Growing
2975 BC
Pyramid
Building 2613-2490
2000 BC
Valley of the Kings
1539–1075 BC
1000 BC
Petra
400-200 BC
Terracota Warriors
246 BC
Colloseum
72 AD
AD 1
Great Wall of China
680 BC - 1681 AC. It took over
2300 years to complete
First gas run vehicle
1886. Ford's mass
production of Cars
1908-1927
Methusaleh Tree
is still growing
AD 1000
AD 2000
Machu Picchu
1450
Taj Mahal
1630

Where Do They Live?

Bristlecone pine trees live in high elevations close to the tree line in some of the harshest conditions found on earth. They live where there is high wind, where it is cold with little sun, and where lightning strikes are common.   The growing season is only six to twelve weeks long.

35

Why Do They Grow So Big and Live So Long in Such Harsh Conditions?

'Amazingly enough adapting to harsh conditions is what helps bristlecone pine trees live so long.

1. During the extremely cold, long winters they enter a dormant state where they use less water, require less sunlight, and generally sleep until summer returns. This makes their growth rings small but strong and resinous.
2. Their wood is strong because of dense, slow growth. This dense wood means that the wood doesn't decay even when dead but is changed by erosion from wind and ice.
3. There is little competition for nutrients in the alkaline limestone soil broken off from limestone boulders they are surrounded by. This makes it so fires are less common.
4. Potential pests that eat pine trees lower down the mountain don't generally travel up the mountain to where they live.
5. The trees can be alive with only a 10-inch strip of bark still growing.
6. The tree is divided into sections with each section having roots. Thus part of the tree can be dead while another part is still alive.

Patriarch is one of the largest bristlecone pine trees found so far. Though it's huge, it is only 1,568 years old which is 3,232 years younger than Methusaleh Bristlecone.

36

They've also adapted to the short growing season by growing extremely dense, resinous wood. Most trees grow over a hundred times faster than bristlecone pine do but over thousands of years the incremental growth adds up. The strong wood deters hungry pine beetles or other folivores from munching on the rock-like trees. It is also makes them more fire resistant. Instead of decaying, they continue standing like amazing statues for hundreds of years. Erosion forces such as blowing rock and ice crystals carve, shape, and twist both living and dead trees.

Unlike other trees that might be killed by one lightning strike, their trunks are divided into different thin sections that carry nutrients to each part of the tree separately from the other parts.   This allows a tree with only a small ten-inch strip of intact bark to still have living branches even when the rest of the tree is dead.

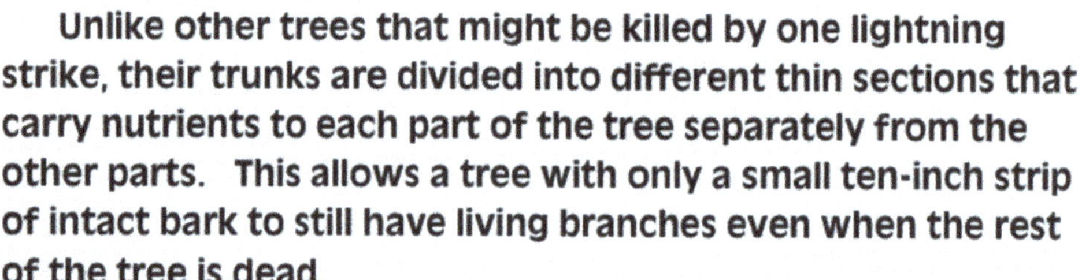

PINE CONES AND PINE NEEDLES

Young Purple pine cones, and reddish buds

Purple pine cones and reddish buds are two unique features of bristlecone pine trees. The purple of the young cones helps them absorb the sun's warmth during the short growing season. The cones turn brown as they mature. Each of the cones' scales have a tip that looks like a little claw or bristle which is where the pine tree derived its name.

Young Purple pine cones,

Unusual pine needles help these trees survive in harsh conditions. Individual pine needles are really bundles of five needles growing from the same <u>fascicle</u> or point on the branch. These needle bundles help provide consistent photosynthesis for the tree during the short growing season. Pine needles can survive for 30 to 45 years. White resin on the needles appears when individual needles in the bundle break off.

Needle Bundles

white resin flakes